First Crush

By

Chris Mabrey

DEDICATION

This book is dedicated to those who believe that it is never too late to change. Many of my patients come to me looking for answers, many of the answers they seek come from within. When they open their minds, hearts and souls to change transformation occurs and their lives are transformed.

FIRST CRUSH

By Chris Mabrey

Flipidy flap, crickedy crack.
Believe me when I tell you girls are wack!

They smell like yucky flowers
and need to take lots of showers.

Girls wear icky lip-gloss and always want to be the boss.

They play dumb games like four square and jump rope and wash their hands with lotion and soap.

They like to wear dresses and make really big messes.

I wish all girls in school would just disappear.
Then all of the boys could rule the school all year.

Boys would be better if girls weren't on earth. It's just how I feel, take it for what its worth.

"Attention students," said my teacher Mrs. Bass. "Please welcome our newest student, Nancy Smith, to our class."

When I first saw her, it was such a surprise.
Nancy Smith was pretty; I could not believe my eyes.

Oh my goodness, my stomach's feeling uneasy—
a little upset, and a little bit queezy!

Why in the world do I feel so strange?
My opinion of girls might have to change.

I must be dreaming; I can't be awake.
I've changed my mind; I've made a mistake.

She has pretty brown pigtails and rosy red cheeks.
This new girl in class I simply must meet.

She has a small little nose and a smile so wide.
But the way that I feel I think I should hide.

My head's going crazy; my mind's in a spin.
"Hello Nancy, I'm Michael. Would you like to use my pen?"

My nose is running; my hair is a mess.
My heart is beating fast, and I cannot catch my breath.

I'm not sick; she's a gift from above.
No, I'm not crazy; this must be what people call love!

My dad always said this day would arrive.
"Me like a girl?" I'd said. "Not while I'm alive."

Now I must tell my dad that what he said was right. He will have to explain my feelings at the dinner table tonight.

Those words I said earlier, I said in a rush.
Who would guess that Nancy Smith would be my first crush.

ABOUT THE AUTHOR

Christopher Mabrey was born in Toledo, Ohio and graduated from St. Francis de Sales High School. He received his Bachelor's Degree in Communications from the University of Toledo, his Master's Degree in Communication and Information Sciences from Ball State University and his Master's Degree in School Counseling from Butler University. Chris Mabrey is a children's book author that has a passion for empowering youth. Through his stories he hopes to encourage his readers to pursue their dreams and excel in life. That is his mission and the catalyst for writing and self-publishing children's books. He is a Licensed Mental Health Therapist who spent several years as a school counselor in Indianapolis, Indiana. He has been a mentor to young people, and has read his books for children at schools and Community Centers. He was given the John E. Worthen award for Outstanding Contribution to Education in 2018. Presently, Christopher works at HealthNet as a Mental Health Therapist.

CPSIA information can be obtained
at www.ICGtesting.com
Printed in the USA
LVHW021109251022
731429LV00010B/108